For Stefan, whose ideas always count.
And for Pierr, who knows how to play. — C. L. S.

To Lynn and Rick and their wonder dog, Mercury,
to Terri and our sunset ride on the big wheel,
and to my brother, Bogue, who always
keeps things rolling. — P. M.

Text copyright © 2003 by Carole Lexa Schaefer
Illustrations copyright © 2003 by Pierr Morgan

First edition 2003

Library of Congress Cataloging-in-Publication Data

Schaefer, Carole Lexa.
One wheel wobbles / by Carole Lexa Schaefer ;
illustrated by Pierr Morgan. — 1st ed.
p. cm.
Summary: Family members parade their favorite types of wheels,
from one wheelbarrow to ten cartwheels.
ISBN 0-7636-0472-0
[1. Wheels—Fiction. 2. Counting.] I. Morgan, Pierr, ill. II. Title.
PZ7.S3315 On 2003
[E]—dc21 2001043762

2 4 6 8 10 9 7 5 3 1

Printed in Italy

This book was typeset in Alghera.
The illustrations were done in ink and gouache resist.

Candlewick Press
2067 Massachusetts Avenue
Cambridge, Massachusetts 02140

visit us at www.candlewick.com

# ONE WHEEL WOBBLES

Carole Lexa Schaefer

illustrated by
Pierr Morgan

CANDLEWICK PRESS
CAMBRIDGE, MASSACHUSETTS

# One wheel wobbles
on Mama's old wheelbarrow.

1

Two wheels spin
on Gramma's
putt-putt motorcycle.

# 3

Three wheels go lickety-split
on Sister's shiny trike.

Four wheels
poke along
on Goatie's
jiggly cart.

4

# 5

Five wheels
sparkle
on Brother's
rainbow-
painted bus.

Six wheels rumble
on Daddy's flatbed truck.

Seven wheels
whirl on Cousin's
classy go-mobile.

7

**8**

Eight wheels zoom
on Grampa's snazzy skates.

9

Nine starry
pinwheels
whir on our
Parade Day
lawn.

And with the turn
of my ten cartwheels...

whoopity

duppity

zippety

zeee!

10

our family parade gets rolling...

... to the biggest
wheel of all!